Tina Marie's ~~Best~~ ~~Worst~~ CHRISTMAS

written by CLARE MISHICA
illustrated by SHEILA LUCAS

for Joel

The Standard Publishing Company, Cincinnati, Ohio. A division of Standex International Corporation.
© 1999 by The Standard Publishing Company. Bean Sprouts™ and the Bean Sprouts design logo are trademarks of
Standard Publishing. Printed in the United States of America.
All rights reserved. Cover design by Robert Glover.

06 05 04 03 02 01 00 99   5 4 3 2 1

Library of Congress Catalog Card Number 99-70916
ISBN 0-7847-1046-5

Standard
Publishing
Cincinnati, Ohio

My Aunt Ella sent me a Christmas present and
Mama said I could open it. I had asked for one
tiny puppy, but I got purple socks and Grandma
sent me pajamas with purple hippos.

"I hate purple," I told Mama.

She said, "Tina Marie, you write two nice thank-you notes." It was going to be the worst Christmas ever.

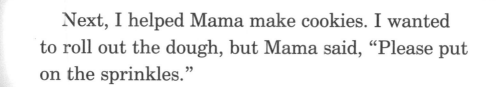

Next, I helped Mama make cookies. I wanted
to roll out the dough, but Mama said, "Please put
on the sprinkles."

After all my hard work, my big brother, Ben, ate every reindeer cookie, so I had to eat a plain old bell.

It was going to be the worst Christmas ever.

Then our family decorated the Christmas tree, and I had to hang my ornaments on the bottom branches.

"I can put the blinking star on top," I told Daddy, and I climbed up onto a chair.

He said, "Tina Marie, please get down before you break your neck!"

Ben put the star on top. He was even allowed to climb a ladder. Ben's allowed to do everything, and he never breaks his neck.

Later, we went caroling. Mama made me wear a long purple scarf, so I wouldn't get cold.

"I hate purple," I told Mama, because she didn't remember.

A minute later, I tripped over that scarf and fell in a snowbank. The snow melted down my back like little icy rivers.

It was going to be the worst Christmas ever.

Finally, the day came for my Sunday school class to put on the Christmas pageant at church. I wanted to be an angel and sing "Glory to God," but I was just a sheep who said "Baaa."

My sheep costume had crooked ears and made my legs itch. Right before I walked on stage, Mama put a bow in my hair. It was purple.

In our manger, we had a real live Baby Jesus. He was my friend Kelly's baby brother, but I don't think he liked playing the part of Jesus. First he cried a little. Then he cried a lot.

"This is the worst Christmas ever," I whispered to a shepherd who had his belt tangled around his feet.

Soon Mary and Joseph started crying too, and I decided that I better say my line before the play ended.

I sucked in a big breath and blurted out
"BAAA!" so loud that even old Mr. Wilby looked
up, and he usually sleeps through everything.

Baby Jesus stopped crying. I said, "Baaa!"
again, and he giggled. Then I walked closer and
squeaked a tiny little "Baaa," just for Baby
Jesus, and he laughed out loud.

I gave Baby Jesus a hug. His cheek felt
softer than Mama's red velvet dress, and his
curls tickled my nose like dandelion fluff.
   He smiled at me, and I forgot all about
purple socks and hippo pajamas,
   plain old bell cookies, bottom branches,
   icy snow down my back, and being a
      sheep who just said "Baaa." Because when
      you hug Baby Jesus—even if it's really
         Kelly's baby brother—you remember
         that Jesus is the best present in the
         whole wide world.

All at once, the angels started singing, and I let Baby Jesus hold my finger so he wouldn't be afraid.

Then everyone stood up and clapped, but they clapped the very loudest when I bowed.

That night, I wore my purple hippo pajamas to bed. They were the same color as the purple duck pajamas that Baby Jesus wore during our pageant.

"Purple's my new favorite color," I told Mama as she kissed me good night.

"I'll remember that," Mama said. "I love you."

"I love you, too," I said.

It was the ~~worst~~ BEST Christmas ever.